The Butler

By
Emma J. Nobis

DISCLAIMER

This story is for adults only. It is written to arouse and entertain. Do not read this story if you are offended by explicit descriptions of adults engaging in various forms of consensual sex.

This is a work of sci-fi. Names, characters, places, and incidents are either the product of the author's imagination or are used fictitiously, and any resemblance to actual persons, living or dead, business establishments, events, or location is entirely coincidental.

COPYRIGHT

Table of Contents

CHAPTER ONE

"Roommate to share a two-bedroom Chicago Gold Coast condo. Please reply by email with résumé and references. Rent negotiable."

Jim answered the Craigslist ad. His lease was up. He thought a change would be good. A new place might get him out of his rut. He rarely left his Humboldt Park apartment except for work and groceries. Living with someone might alter his morose attitude.

It was unusual for him to take action like this, to make a change in his life. Normally, he went about his day without a plan or purpose. The highlight of his week was always a moment he could help someone out. He likes Chicago winters because it presented the opportunity to help push a car out of a snowbank.

But feeling good didn't drive him to make a change in his life. No, it was the insistent, nagging dread of meaninglessness. He saw her ad because he read Craigslist for entertainment. He read Craigslist personals for something to do; it gave him an insight into people who had lives.

He sent his one-page résumé, such as it was. The interview was brief, ten minutes on a Saturday morning. He met her in a law office in the loop. Jennifer Kendall was trim, tall, attractive, and purposeful. Her efficient demeanor was consistent with her position as a fourth-year associate in a large multinational law firm.

He was not entirely clear why she chose him. First of all, he's two decades older than her. Second, he's not in her class: she, a high-power attorney, he, a warehouse manager. He didn't even own a suit.

Women, especially like her, never notice him. And he is not comfortable in a room of men attracted to her. Still, he moved in the first of the following month. She made the rent affordable on his salary. "What the heck?" he thought.

Six days a week, she woke up very early, went to the health club in the building, and returned for a shower and light breakfast. She took the bus to the loop, arriving at her office before 7:00. Most evenings she was in bed at 9:00. He accommodated his life to her schedule. The third morning he made coffee while she was in the shower. She smiled when she appeared in the kitchen and accepted the mug from his hand. He liked the smile. To him, it meant he had been helpful. He liked being helpful.

He took to preparing her granola, yogurt, and dried fruit breakfast. Somehow, it didn't seem right to simply put the cartons out on the kitchen island, so he served each in a Polish pottery bowl with a spoon for her to assemble as she desired.

While wandering around Woodfield Shopping Center on a Sunday morning, he found the Polish pottery set. The blue of the decoration reminded him of her eyes, her intensely blue eyes. Sometimes he had to look away. The intensity of her eyes, he thought, would make her intimidating at depositions.

He purchased an insulated carafe for her coffee. She sometimes liked to add cream. He kept a small pitcher in the refrigerator so it would stay cold. Each of these extras he added one at a time, as he thought of them.

It felt right to please her, to be helpful. He found he liked making things right. He stepped out of his negative attitude by thinking of small things he might do for her. Her smile encouraged him. Life was better, living with her. He did well in this move, even if his commute was longer. Things at work seemed to pick up as well. He was happy.

Their little morning ritual began when she walked into the kitchen, fresh from her shower, dressed for the office. He'd hand her the mug. She would smile. A gentle "Good morning" from her was the perfect start to his day. He would then leave her to her thoughts and preparations for the day.

After his shower, he put her dishes in the dishwasher and drove to his warehouse management job. He needed to be at work at 9:00, so there was plenty of time. He liked the physical act of cleaning up after her. She deserved it. She worked hard. He could see she would be an important attorney.

He parked in her spot in the building. She didn't need a car. Once in a while, when she had an errand to run on a weekend, he would drive her to her destination and wait for her to return. Waiting was easier than finding a parking space on the street. He didn't mind.

He appreciated being near her. It was clearly stated there would be no sexual connection between them. She set the boundaries and he respected them. In his early twenties, he might have imagined a relationship would blossom. But years have gone by. He had a good job, nothing like hers, but still with decent pay. He was going nowhere special. He went to work each day and back home. He had not gone on an actual date in years. No one was interested. He accepted that.

Wednesday mornings were his "late day." One manager needed to be present for evening hours. His night was Wednesday. He didn't go in until two. The second week he lived with her, he got out of the vacuum and did the carpets. He hesitated at the door to her room. He did not open it. The following Sunday afternoon, he explained his schedule and asked if she would like him to vacuum her room. She smiled. "Why James! That would be so kind of you."

He cleaned her room, straightening the side chairs by the window. He was going to do his laundry, washing his sheets anyway, so he stripped her bed and remade it with sheets he found in her linen closet. He washed her sheets with his, folded them, and returned them to her linen closet. The next morning, along with her smile, came a gentle "thank you." It made his day. Her expression of appreciation for some little thing he did made him almost dizzy.

It wasn't long before he added cleaning her bathroom to his Wednesday morning routine. None of this was a lot to do, and he enjoyed that morning smile. One Thursday she had an early breakfast meeting. The entire schedule was off, with no coffee this morning. As she left to catch a cab, she asked if he would be "so good" as to make her bed that morning. He said, "of course." She smiled; he closed the door behind her.

He began making her bed every morning except Sunday. On Saturday evenings she often had a "gentleman caller" who stayed the night. When that happened, Jim stayed out of the way, enjoying a late morning in bed himself, or going out early for a leisurely breakfast. This is why he was wandering about the mall on a Sunday purchasing pottery. She should have her space and he made way for her.

He didn't think too much about the men who stayed the night. He seldom saw them. He didn't like meeting them. It wasn't jealousy, but a deep unease about what they might think of him. He feared their scorn and laughter about his age and chaste existence.

Some of those who stayed the night were not quiet. He could hear them in her bedroom groaning. Once in a while, he heard a visitor cry out. He didn't think about it. He would be there when they were gone. Besides, so far as he could tell, she rarely brought the same one home more than twice, and only on Saturday night. He thought these men, while they had access to her bed, could not substitute for his service to her. Life was good.

Yet it seems nothing remains perfect forever. On a particularly stormy Monday morning, he overslept. A clap of thunder woke him up. He had no idea what had happened. He may have shut off the alarm instead of hitting snooze. More likely he failed to set the alarm the night before. Either way, he rushed out only to see her at the door. She asked if he was ill. When he said he wasn't, she said, "I'll get coffee on my way to the office." There was no smile. The door closed.

Her dishes were rinsed and in the dishwasher. Her bed was already made. He sat down in the side chair by the window in her room and cried. Feelings of loss and guilt came over him. He vowed it would not happen again, but he could not get over his overwhelming sense of shame. He failed; there was no smile.

The next morning, as he handed her the mug, he apologized for oversleeping, for ruining the peace of her morning. He could not look at her face. He feared her eyes, finding disappointment and judgment in them. He didn't look up on Wednesday morning either, only at the floor and her shoes. She put her hand under his chin and lifted his face. "I know you feel bad. Don't worry. Let's talk about this on Sunday morning when we both have time."

But he did worry about it. He had no idea what Sunday morning would bring. He worked extra hard cleaning the whole apartment. Thursday morning, she said, "Nice job." He could not look at her.

Saturday evening, she came back late after going out, but there was no one with her. Sunday morning at 8:00 there was a knock on his door. "It's time for our talk." He pulled on some clothes and joined her in the living room.

She was dressed for the health club. Lycra shorts, matching fitted top, hair pulled back, he enjoyed her workout clothes. But this morning they were going to talk about his failure. He put his head down. "Tell me what happened on Monday morning."

"I overslept; my alarm didn't go off." He apologized. "I feel awful about it."

"I know. I know you felt remorse, and you continue to feel that way. Mistakes happen, I'm ready to move on. But you don't seem prepared to get past it."

He was honest with her, "I just don't know what to say. I have trouble even looking at you. I don't know how to 'get past' Monday. I used to get this way when I lived alone. One mistake would live with me for weeks. I don't know how to make it up. Never have."

"Perhaps you can't 'make it up,' but you can pay for a mistake. By paying for it, you can leave it behind and be free of shame. Once a criminal has done his time, he has paid his debt to society. He is freed. He is let out of prison. Might it be like that for you? Might you be free of your prison of shame?"

"How can I pay for it?"

"Maybe some kind of punishment for your mistake would get us past this dark attitude of yours."

He looked down and asked, "What kind of punishment?"

"Well, if I were to give you a spanking, once we were done, the air would be cleared, and you could look me in the eye once more. We would never have to speak of it ever again."

He looked up, then down again. "You would give me a spanking?"

"Yes, right now, this morning, if it would clear the air and we could get back to our normal routine without all this apologizing all the time."

He didn't know what to say. He didn't move. He was frozen in his seat. She stood up and said, "Follow me."

The Butler

In a fog, he followed into her bedroom. He later remembered the curve of her hips highlighted by tight lycra. His mind was blank, he wanted to touch her. He wanted to get on his knees and say he was sorry. She stopped at the chair by the window. "Go to my dresser, get the hairbrush, hand it to me."

He dusted her dresser many times and moved this hairbrush. It was black wood and heavy. It may have been an antique. The rounded backside had an inlaid flower design. He wondered about it. He didn't think she used it to brush her hair. The thought had occurred to him that it would make a great spanking implement. He had often wondered what it would be like to be spanked; now he was going to find out. He gave the brush to her.

Bending over her knee was awkward. Having her pull down his underwear was embarrassing. Head down, he could see only her running shoes and ankles. The spanking really was painful and, as predicted, cathartic. Standing in the corner of her bedroom, trousers around his ankles, hands behind his head, bottom feeling hot and heavy and very naked, she gave him time for the experience to take effect. She surfed the morning news. After what seemed like a long time, she said, "You may now pull up your pants. Please sit in the chair."

He did what he was told, sat, and looked at her. She smiled. "I see all has been made right. My grandmother's hairbrush still works wonders. We won't speak of this again." She left and went to the health club. He made her bed and went back to his own, exhausted. He slept until noon.

Examining himself in the mirror, he found only one small bruise on his right buttock. This lack of markings was surprising because the spanking hurt. It hurt so much more than he might have expected. He had trouble staying on her lap. She stopped once and made him bend over one leg so she could hold him down with the other. At the time, he felt completely overwhelmed, and, as a result, now thoroughly freed of his shame.

Spanking had long been a part of his fantasy life. It was like an old friend, always there. Most pornography he had seen involving spanking had a man spanking a woman. This made no sense to him. If the stronger one spanked the weaker, it just seemed like abuse to him. No, being spanked by a woman made more sense. It was the amount of pain that was unexpected. A spanking from her hairbrush really hurt.

Her smile returned, or rather he was able to see her smile again. They never spoke about his failures because there was a new ritual. Whenever he felt he disappointed her in some way, her grandmother's hairbrush worked its magic. There would come a knock on his door and they would have their "little talk." He always felt better after and she seemed to enjoy providing his spanking.

The Butler

He came to treasure his corner time. Not because he stood semi-naked in her bedroom, but because of the pleasure she exhibited when she released him. Standing in the corner was the essence of his punishment; his moment of transition. Perhaps, the awful spanking put him in the right place to wait for her release, "Please pull up your pants, come here and sit down." It all made perfect sense to him. He was very happy.

She told him the hairbrush was precious to her. It was a part of her family's history. She thought it may have been her great-grandmother's. If so, it would have been used to correct her grandmother. She was certain her grandmother used it to spank her mother. Her own mother used it on her when she was a teen. It was now unused, unlikely to spank another teenager.

That was something to ponder. Generations of women used that brush to spank younger women in their family. Now, she used the back of the same hairbrush on him. He thought about those female bottoms every time he dusted her room and rearranged the top of her dresser. The hairbrush itself chased all other thoughts and shame from his head when she used it on him. It became precious to him as well.

He spent the next two very happy years serving her, making her life better and staying out of her way. When her firm promoted her, he rejoiced with her. When she made a junior partner, she moved to a larger condo on the upper floor. It included a 'maid's room' built next to the kitchen. That became his room.

CHAPTER TWO

Their cathartic spankings became a monthly ritual. Maintenance spankings, as she called them, provided all the intimacy he needed. Over her knee, the complexities of the life dissolved into the rhythm of the hairbrush and bottom; in ouch and corner time he felt peace. Standing in the corner of her room felt right, everything in order. He never did, however, get over how much her spankings hurt. It was always a struggle to stay on her lap, but he knew it was where he belonged.

He worked to fit into her life, taking care of her home. When his company downsized, he lost his warehouse manager position. She reduced his rent while he sought another job that fit her schedule. Rather than feeling sorry for himself, his focus became maintaining her condo and making life easier for her. Paradoxically, it seemed, he was emotionally stronger the more he served. He found his purpose in her home.

As she advanced in her career, he felt no little pride in her accomplishments. Not that she spoke in-depth with him about her job, but he could tell when she excelled. It made him feel good to think he played some small part.

While out of work, he took classes, learning to cook. He made dinner for her. He was delighted when she complimented him on his use of seasoning and spices. Everything was going well, very well, until that day. The day that changed everything.

The day he still didn't speak of was the day she discovered his secret. There is always a secret. Everyone has one. But he involved her, making the situation intolerable. When she found out his secret, it was devastating.

Every morning, after he made her bed, he would pick up anything out of place. Once in a while she left something, perhaps a jacket, on the back of her side chair, or a skirt folded on the seat. He hung them up in her closet. It was not difficult to understand where these should go.

A year ago, not long after they moved into the new condo, he found a knit top on the foot of the bed. He wondered if it should be folded in a drawer or hung up. He opened the drawers in her room to see if that was where it should go. What he saw was her collection of lingerie and undergarments. He hung the knit top in the closet.

That evening he asked if that was the right place. She pointed to some shelves built into the back of the closet. He folded the top and put it next to the sweaters there. It should have been obvious. She laughed. He laughed, "I must be blind."

But the damage had been done. He was not blind; he had seen her undergarments. He couldn't forget. Of course, he knew they were there. Of course, he knew she wore underwear, bras, stocking, lingerie. But now he had seen it. The following Wednesday morning, after making the bed and cleaning her bath, he opened that top drawer. He could smell her presence. Things have been moving. He could tell what she had worn that week.

Wednesday mornings became very special to him. He would open all three drawers of her dresser, one at a time. Silently observing which items she tended to wear most often. He didn't touch anything. He memorized each item and its placement in her dresser drawers. Each Wednesday he carefully closed the drawers and returned to his room. He enjoyed "pleasuring himself" in the shower before going to work.

He made it a rule never to open any drawer until all his tasks for the morning were accomplished. He limited his enjoyment to just looking, memorizing, and speculating on what she would wear that week. And, very importantly, only on Wednesday morning after he cleaned her room.

He made her bed and put away any clothes lying about. He cleaned the bath, wiped down the glass shower door, and polished the chrome fixtures till they sparkled. He dusted, straightened, and vacuumed her bedroom. He lovingly arranged her grandmother's hairbrush with the other items on her dresser. Only then, after being very careful to do the best job possible, would he allow himself a long, silent peek.

21

Slowly pulling open the first drawer, inhaling her scent, guessing which items she might wear, these were heady moments. He did not touch, but he did lean in to get his nose close. It was a silent ritual; opening and closing one drawer at a time. Nothing disturbed, nothing out of place, nothing touched, he rationalized his indulgence.

He looked forward to his Wednesday ritual, even more than his monthly spankings. Other days of the week were for cleaning the kitchen, or the living room. On Wednesdays he cleaned her room. Only on Wednesdays would he open those three drawers of stockings and underwear and bras, her lingerie and stockings.

On Wednesdays, in a long hot shower, he relished thinking about those stockings, that chemise, perhaps her lace brassiere on her. And he was happy, very, very happy.

Happy until one Wednesday morning she came home unexpectedly. She observed him in her room with his head in her underwear drawer. She watched his little ritual. Opening each drawer, savoring the contents, and closing it. He turned to walk out and there she was.

He froze. Nothing good could come of this. His secret was exposed. "Um, how long have you been home?"

"Long enough, it seems."

The Butler

"I didn't expect to see you there. You startled me."
"Just what were you doing in my dresser?"

"Um, I cleaned your room."

"And you cleaned my underwear?"

"No, no, no. I didn't touch what was in those drawers."

"I see. You just looked and didn't touch it."

"Yes. I never touch your things except to clean or put them away. I would never touch what is in those drawers."

"I think you better go to your room now, and don't come back here."

He trudged off to his room. She did not move as he approached her in the hall. He feared those eyes. He could not look at her. He could tell she was upset. There was no smile. He had to turn sideways to get by her. He went to his room, then left for work by the back door.

Thursday morning, he apologized as he handed her the coffee mug. His secret ritual, once discovered, broke something. No apology was enough. He hung his head and waited for the inevitable. He knew even a Sunday spanking was not going to fix it.

"We will discuss this Sunday morning. I will think about consequences. You have betrayed my trust and violated my sense of security in my home. Changes will be made. Until then, I do not want to see you. You will remain in your room when I am here and use only the back door."

He read between the lines. He might not have a place to live on Sunday evening. Two of the happiest years of his life were destroyed by one act of selfish indulgence. He trudged off to his room. After she left for work, he cleaned up the kitchen. He did not go into her room. He didn't know whether her bed was made or not.

He felt lost and it was his own fault. If he hadn't opened those drawers that day, he would still be able to greet her in the morning. On Friday morning, he made the coffee, set out the breakfast, and hid in his room until he heard her leave for the office.

Saturday was the same. She was gone most of the day. She returned only to go out for the evening. He tried to avoid being in her presence as she asked. The condo was impeccably clean, he saw it. He did not go into her room.

Sunday morning arrived. At 8:00 there was that dreaded knock on his door. He had been awake for hours. He was terrified. This talk could mean having to move out. He followed her, not to her room as usual, but to the dining room table. He was surprised to find another woman there.

She was short, stocky, and older, maybe 60? Her grey hair was pulled back in a bun. She greeted him with a handshake. "My name is JoEllen Lake. You may call me Miss Lake. You must be James. I am glad to meet you."

He had no idea what she was doing here. Her greeting was disarming. He hesitated, "I'm happy to meet you too, Miss Lake."

"Please, let's be seated," she said, gesturing. Jennifer sat at the head of the table, Miss Lake across from Jim. Her blouse gaped open slightly. Jim looked down.

Jennifer explained, "James, Miss Lake is a consultant, a counselor of sorts. I have invited her to help us sort out our issues and my unexpected feelings of insecurity in my home."

"Yes, James, my job is to help people resolve violations of trust with just and lasting results. I understand Miss Kendall observed you doing something inappropriate. Would you describe for me what you did so I can understand the scope of things?"

Jim stared at her. His mouth was open, but no words came out. She straightened in her chair. Her blouse closed. Her voice suddenly sharp and demanding, "James, what did you do?"

"I have trouble talking about it."

"That is quite alright young man. It can be difficult to admit an injustice that harms another." She paused. Her voice returned to its calm assurance. "Just tell me what you can."
"Miss Jennifer caught me looking at her dresser."

"You like looking, don't you James? Just like you like looking at my blouse?"

"No, I wasn't. I'm not looking." He quickly looked down at the table.

"You weren't just looking at Miss Kendall's dresser, were you, James."

"Yes, I was just looking and smelling. I didn't touch anything. I never do."

"Ah, this isn't the only time, is it James?"

"No, but I never touch anything."

"This was the only time she caught you, wasn't it?"

"Yes."

"And you never touch anything of hers."

"Nothing in those drawers. I make her bed and hang up her clothes. But nothing in those drawers."

"You don't touch her intimate things, but you do touch yours, don't you James."

"What do you mean?"

"After looking, you masturbate, don't you James?"
He just looked down at the table again. He felt a
flush on his neck. "It's OK, James. Masturbating is
not a crime. Everyone does it. Do you masturbate
after looking at Miss Kendall's underwear?"

"Yes."

"Can you understand how that might make her feel
uncomfortable?"

"I never meant any harm. I only looked."

"And you masturbated."

He continued to examine one small area of the
wooden table. He dared not to look up. "And you
masturbate after examining her underwear?" Her
voice sharped and demanding again.

"Yes."

"Thank you, James, for helping us understand. You
do enjoy looking at women's underthings. We have
observed you enjoying the occasional glimpse of a
bra when you think women are unaware. And now,
with proximity to her clothing, you have been
enjoying unfettered peeks at Miss Kendall's
underwear while she is not here." There was a
pause. "Now, how long have you lived here?" Her
gentle voice returned.

"Here for almost a year. In her smaller condo a bit more than a year ago."

"So, two years?"

"Yes." He brightened and looked up.

"And just how long have you been masturbating after looking at Miss Kendall's underwear?

His head went down again. "How long, James?"

"Less than a year."

"I see: for months now, you have enjoyed yourself at Miss Kendall's expense, and without her knowledge or permission."

"Yes." When she put it that way, it didn't sound so innocuous. He knew it was bad. He didn't know how bad it was.

"I see." Jennifer remained quiet the whole time, but now she spoke. "For months now?"

"You see, Miss Kendall, James believed his masturbation was not hurting you. His trigger, your underwear, was untouched, so he thought it was OK. He rationalized his actions, not considering his violation of your person. I am curious, James. Did you imagine what it would be like to wear Miss Kendall's underwear? Did you imagine putting on Miss Kendall's underwear while masturbating?"

"Oh no! No, I only imagined it on her, never on me."

"Ah, then you pictured Miss Kendall in her underwear as you masturbated."

After a long pause, he said, "Yes."

"Thank you for giving us a picture of your deviance, Mr. O'Neall." She paused and reflected for a moment. James just looked at the table.

"You enjoy looking at models in lingerie ads, don't you James? You always have, haven't you?"

He looked up. "Yes, but isn't that what they are for, to look at?"

"I expect you borrowed your mother's magazines and enjoyed pictures of models in the ads for intimate apparel? Let me guess. You are right-handed, but you use your left hand to masturbate, don't you Mr. O'Neall?"

"I... What?"

"After you look in Miss Kendall's underwear drawers, you masturbate using your left hand. It feels odd to use your right."

Jim looked down at his hands. "How did you know that?"

Ignoring his question, she went on. "Can you understand how Miss Kendall might be concerned about your behavior and your continued unsupervised presence in her apartment?"

Jim continued to stare at this woman who seemed to know more about him than anyone. But they just met. He had prepared his answer to this question beforehand. "Well, yes. I have thought about it. If she wants me to leave, it will take an hour for me to pack."

"James, I don't want you to leave. Your service has been very helpful. It would be difficult to replace you. I have researched options for the past few days, and I found Miss Lake. I think she will be able to assist in allowing me to feel safe and in adjudicating our situation. If you would like to stay, please hear her out."

There was a long pause. Jim looked at each woman, sighed, and said, "I would like to stay. It won't happen again."

"Very good, James. But I think we need to examine the whole situation. First, there is Miss Kendall's justifiable concern about leaving you unsupervised in her apartment. The basis of that concern is masturbation while fantasizing about her underwear. Your fantasy goes way back to when you held those magazine ads in your right hand while masturbating with your left.

You have fetishized women's underwear because women's bodies are inaccessible to you."

She continued turning to Jennifer. "Fetishes like this are difficult to stop with willpower alone. James may want to stop, but he will need help."

She turned back to Jim. "I believe a twofold solution is in order. First, if you regularly wash her underwear and lingerie by hand, it will lose its exotic appeal. Are you willing to wash her underwear weekly and return it folded to its appropriate place as needed?"

Jim started at her a long while before venturing an affirmation. This plan was totally unexpected. He would stay up all hours, if needed, to wash what he had never dared touch.

"Then there is the matter of masturbation. After you wash, dry, and fold her underwear, will you promise not to masturbate in response? Remember, it will be hanging in your bathroom to dry before you fold it."

"I promise not to masturbate." Jim could not believe his ears. Jennifer's bras were hanging in his bath. He could not get the image out of his mind. He felt an erection growing. He shifted in his seat.

"Ah, I see this has made you uncomfortable. It is easy to say you won't masturbate, but we both know you will have difficulty keeping your promise. I have something to help with that."

She reached down into her bag and brought it two boxes. One said "CB 6000," the other "CB 6000s." At the bottom of the box, both said, "Male Chastity Device."

"These are chastity devices. They work by locking up your penis and preventing contact. Either of these will help you keep your promise. You won't be able to masturbate. Wearing one of these will relieve Miss Kendall of her concern about your behavior during the unsupervised time in her apartment. What do you think?"

"Um, I don't know."

"They don't hurt in any way but can take some time to get used to wearing them. The CB6000 is a normal size. The CB6000s is the small size. Either is effective if worn continually. After a few days, you will forget you have it on. Care must be taken to keep it clean. It also may chafe. A silicon-based lubricant eases this issue."

"Um, is there another option?"

"I don't know of one, other than to move out, which neither of you desires. Why don't you go try one on? Just take them to your room and follow the instructions. Here is an extra tube of lubricant."

"Well, OK." He went to his room and opened the normal-sized one. There were a lot of parts. He read the instructions and saw how the parts went together. There were several sizes of rings and spacers. There was a knock at his door.

"Would you like some help with it? I am quite good at fitting one of those." The door slowly opened. Miss Lake had on medical gloves. "Let's get you ready."

She laid out the five rings, spacers, and posts. "OK, let's see what we've got to work with. Please pull your pants down." She sat down on the bed. He stood before her. "Oh yes, I believe the smaller size is right for you."

After testing the two smaller rings, she decided on the middle size. She lubricated it and put it on around his cock and balls. With practiced ease, she assembled the rest of the device using the smallest spacer. The lock went on and he was wearing a chastity device.

"There now. That looks good, and it doesn't hurt at all, does it?"

"Umm, no. But what happens when I need to pee?"

"You just line up the end of your penis with the hole in the tube made for that purpose. The smaller size tube makes it easier to keep the ureter lined up. Most men find it best to sit down to urinate. Less messy that way."

"Always sit down?"

She laughed, "The benefit is that you won't leave the toilet seat up anymore." She paused, then continued, "There are a lot of YouTube videos and discussions about how to keep one of these clean. It is much more common than you might think."
"May I have the keys?"

"No. That would defeat the whole purpose. One key will remain with Miss Kendall in case she sees a need to unlock you. I will have another one. Here is my card in case of an emergency."

"I don't have the key?"

"No, I repeat. The whole point is prevention and safety. Miss Kendall can be confident you are not masturbating while washing out her underwear as long as she has the key, and you don't. Please dress and come back to the table when you are ready."

She left, pulling off her gloves. Jim remained behind, examining his new cage. He could see his member through the clear plastic, but he could not touch it. His balls were trapped between the tube and the ring. He tried twisting and pulling. It was clear this thing was not going to come off easily. He dressed and went back to the dining room. Jennifer was wearing the key to the lock on a gold chain as a necklace.

"Miss Kendall and I have been conferring. She was completely unaware of the length of time you had been in her drawers, so to speak." She chuckled at her little joke. "We feel there will need to be some reckoning for your deviant behavior. What do you think?"

"Jennifer sometimes punishes me for mistakes."

"Oh, the little spankings she gives you? Those are simply warnings. No, a day of reckoning for months of voyeurism and masturbation at her expense involves more than a little over the knee spanking. Miss Kendall is ready to contract with the organization I represent to provide more serious discipline. Are you ready to pay the price for your indiscretions?"

"What organization?"

"Midway Correction and Domination Services. Our office is located near Midway Airport. This division of our organization is entirely female managed and staffed."

"Oh."

"Some use the initials of our company to call us Micky D'S." She laughed again. "We offer custom disciplinary punishment and correction. We are very good at it. Our clients are uniformly pleased with our services. Delinquents, such as yourself, find our methods effective. Miss Kendall is the client, you the delinquent."

"Jennifer would contract with you to punish me for..."

Suddenly serious, Miss Lake continued, "Miss Kendall, the client, contracts with Mickey D'S to provide discipline for you to an extent agreed by all three of us. At the appointed time, you come to our office and one of our expert staff provides the appropriate correction. Justice is served. You go home. If there is a necessary follow up, you can make an appointment before you leave. It is all quite simple."

"James, I am very aware of how important your spankings have become to you and to me. I see no reason to stop spanking you on a regular basis. But this is different. For months you have kept this erotic fantasy secret involving me. Early on, we might have dealt with it together. But now it has gone past that. This is the best solution I could find. I think we should work with them."

Miss Lake jumped in, "I have our standard contract here. All we have to fill in is the level of punishment, the means and the appointment time. Everything else is prepared according to my preliminary conversations with Miss Kendall."

Jennifer took the contract and started reading. She was a lawyer, contract law was her specialty. She was satisfied. "Not the way I would have written it, but it will suffice."

Jim read his copy. Three pages of small print. On the first page he saw he had a voice in the contract, if he agreed to it. He would receive corporal punishment, he could choose the implement, Jennifer the level or extent of the punishment. Additional punishments, if any, would be decided by agreement with his disciplinarian at the time of his appointment.

"What level, Miss Kendall? I think James' delinquency deserves a severe penalty, don't you?" "You have more experience of these things. Severe. Level five?"

1, 2, and 3 are considered warnings, 4, 5, and 6 are reprimands, 7, 8, and 9 are severe, 10 and up are judicial. For first-timers, we don't recommend anything beyond severe. May I suggest a level 7 in this case?"

"Level seven it is, don't you agree, James?"

"Um, OK." Jim was clearly hesitant.

"James, Miss Kendall, and I agree that a level seven correction will provide justice for her and for you. Do you agree with a level seven corporal punishment? Yes or no?"

"Yes," James replied in a very small voice.

"More enthusiasm, man! Level seven, yes or no?"

"Yes! Level seven!"

"Wonderful! What implement do you select? For a level seven, you can have a leather prison strap, a dragon cane, or a wooden paddle."

"I don't know."

"May I suggest the paddle? It is the most controlled. Your disciplinarian is less likely to have an errant stroke."

"The paddle."

"Now we need to choose the secondary implement, to be used at the discretion of your disciplinarian. You can choose, tawes, or junior cane."

"What's a tawes?"

"It is a leather strap split into two or three tails. In your case, I recommend it over the cane, but either would be effective."

"I'll choose that."

"Which?"

"The leather strap thing."

"Oh, excellent! You have chosen well, Mr. O'Neall! I am so pleased with your cooperation in filing this contract!

She paused and wrote about his choices. "There we have it; A level seven paddling with enhancements, and a tawes for secondary correction. Miss Kendall has already selected all the very best options. She obviously cares about your well-being. Everything will be taken care of. Neither of you has anything to worry about. Miss Kendall, James here will be dealt with appropriately. Mr. O'Neall, your discipline will be carried out safely and effectively. Are there any questions?"

"When will this happen?"
"Oh my, thank you, James. In the excitement, I almost forgot. You have been so very good and compliant. We have an opening on Friday morning. Can you get medical leave for a day from work? A nurse on our staff can provide a letter of confirmation if necessary."

"I can get the day off."

"Wonderful. Your appointment will be at 9:45 in the morning. Please do not be either late or early. We have reserved a six-minute window for your arrival - three minutes on either side of 9:45. You want to arrive at the front door of our office between 9:42 and 9:48. This protects the privacy of other clients and delinquents."

"Other clients." Jim paused. "Will Jennifer be there?"

"No James, you will be on your own. I hope to hear how things went Friday evening when I get home."

"Here are your instructions including directions to our office. Please read these and be on time. I can't emphasize it enough. You want to be on time for this appointment. There will be an additional correction for arriving outside these times. We don't want that."

If it had not been for the chastity cage, he would have been obsessed all week about Friday morning. But the cage between his legs was a more immediate predicament. His continual proximity to Jennifer's lingerie resulted in an almost constant pressure when he was home. At work, sometimes he forgot he was wearing the device, but he found he had to sit to urinate. It was odd not feeling his penis, the plastic tube prevented any contact. At work it was just strange, but he could deal with it.

Jennifer showed him how to wash her things in Woolite. He set up a washbasin on the counter in his bath. He washed, then rinsed each item twice, then hung it up on a clothesline he installed on new hooks across his bath.

He took baths with her bras and underwear hanging over his head. At home, the cage became impossibly frustrating. He learned where to apply the lubricant to reduce irritation. The first night he woke up several times. Thursday morning, he had a painful erection trapped in plastic. Mercifully, Friday morning came quickly.

Jennifer did not exercise on Friday but instead spent the morning with him. She made the coffee before he got up! When she seemed concerned, he told her it would be alright. She should go to work. Not to worry. He liked her smile. He missed seeing it. She put her hand on his shoulder. "We'll talk this evening." He closed the door behind her.

He rinsed the dishes and loaded the dishwasher. He left at 8:00, so he would not be late. An inbound accident on Stevenson caused an outbound backup that completely stopped traffic. Starting early meant he pulled into the parking lot behind the building at about 9:30. He took a breath. He would be on time.

Out the back door of the office building, a nurse was helping a man to his car. He had trouble getting into the driver's seat. He was clearly stiff, requiring assistance to sit. She waved to the other driver as she walked back to the door. The man started his car and drove off. It was 9:40. Jim got out of his car and stretched. Traffic made it a difficult drive.

The yellow brick office building was one story with no windows except in front. It may have been a medical building at one time. The parking lot said Midway CD Services parking only. A privacy hedge surrounded the whole lot. He walked slowly around to the front of the building. The door said MCDS, Inc. He looked at his phone. 9:45. He pushed the button on the intercom.

"May I help you?"

"James O'Neall for my appointment."

The door buzzed. He went inside. There was no one else in the small waiting room. A young, blond-haired woman greeted him from behind the reception desk. "Welcome, Mr. O'Neall. I'm Cynthia. This is your first time here, isn't it?"

"Yes, my first time."

"I have your chart and your contract here. Everything is in order and the team is ready for you. I want to thank you for being on time. It makes my job so much more pleasant. I really hate arguing about the time stamp. I will put you down as arriving punctually at 9:45."

"I'm glad I left early; traffic was a bear."

"Oh, I am so happy you allowed enough time. But if you come in for another appointment, it is not good to sit in the parking lot for so long. I recommend parking on the street close by and driving up at the right time."

Jim looked up at the monitor showing the parking area. "Um, OK. I thought waiting five minutes in the lot was OK."

"It was more like fourteen minutes, Mr. O'Neall. And you should not have observed someone leaving. They deserve their privacy just as you do. Please understand there will be consequences if you enter the lot early again."

"Of course. I'm sorry. I get it."

"Very good, Mr. O'Neall." Her bright voice was disarming. "May I see your photo I.D. so I can verify your identity?"

Jim produced his driver's license. "Very good, Mr. O'Neall," she said as she handed it back. "We never want to give away our discipline to an undeserving person." She chuckled at her own little joke. "Now empty your pockets. Put everything in this tray. Yes, cell phone, wallet, keys. Any change, jewelry, or anything metal? No? You can see that the tray is closed and sealed with this numbered seal. Please sign the inventory here. They will stay locked while we have them. I will see that this tray is returned to you in your exit interview."

She turned and put the tray on a shelf next to five other trays. "A busy morning?" he asked.

"You have no idea." She rolled her eyes. "Your positive attitude is a delight. Sometimes guys who come for disciplinary services can be difficult. My last intake was simply impossible." She pulled out a clipboard with papers. "This is our medical intake form. You may fill it out in our orientation room. Please go through the door to your left."

The door buzzed. He sat in the only chair and began to fill in typical medical questions: prescription medications - none. Over the counter or herbal medications - none. He finished the form and looked around. Across from him was a large screen television. No windows, no other furnishings, just a chair, the TV, and three doors. He looked up and noticed the security camera.

The receptionist came in through the second door. "I see you finished. Very good. You are doing extraordinarily well, Mr. O'Neall. Thank you for being efficient. Makes my day go so much better."

Jim was pleased. He liked being helpful and this pretty receptionist made him feel good about it. Her short tight skirt showed a lot of thighs. He felt the grip of his chastity cage as he admired the curve of her bottom. He shifted in his seat.

"We have a video orientation for you to watch. After that, please sign these final release forms." Handing him another clipboard of papers, she turned on the TV and left him. The door opened for her when she entered the code. The same keypad was next to each door. He realized he was locked in. The video on the monitor started.

"Welcome to Midway Correction and Domination Services. We pride ourselves in offering safe, sane, and consensual discipline in both traditional and contemporary forms." The recording went on to describe, with cartoon graphics, what he could expect to happen. The video was specific to his level seven paddling. It repeatedly emphasized that the staff was professional and highly trained in providing effective consequences for delinquent behaviors.

The tape ended; the light came back on. Jim leafed through the papers and signed or initialed where indicated. He put the clipboard in his lap and waited. The third door opened. A woman in hospital scrubs came in.

"Mr. O'Neall, I am Nurse Lanette. I will be taking you through the next steps in your journey today. How do you feel this morning?"

"OK. That cartoon was a bit scary. I'm a little nervous."

"To be expected. I'll be the one that helps you through the process. You won't be alone. First, let's get you checked out. Won't you follow me?" She held the door open. He followed her down a hall to a medical exam room. The lines of her panties were clearly visible through the tight-fitting scrubs. The door closed. He heard it latched.

She looked through his release forms and added them to his file. "Please undress completely for your exam. You may put your clothes, including your shoes, in this basket. The dressing gown behind you goes on with the back open. I'm sure you have been through this before for medical exams. Any questions? No? Alright, I'll be back." She used the keypad to open the door.

He put his shoes on the bottom of the basket and folded his clothes on top. He never figured out how to tie one of those paper gowns behind his back. The nurse returned and tied it for him. After reviewing his intake forms and checking his vital signs, she said it was time for his enema.

She had him bend over the table. "This keeps things clean in our operating theater. Sometimes delinquents lose control of their bowels. I'll be back in a little bit." She left carrying his clothes with her. The enema brought on cramping. There was a gurgling from his gut and a serious twinge. He tried the door. It was locked.

He was in real pain. It took every ounce of energy he had to keep from expelling all over the exam room. She knocked twice and held the door open. "Sorry, there was another delinquent in the hall. I had to wait for the hall to be clear. The toilet is the first door on the left." He moved quickly and relieved himself.

He was escorted back to the exam room. She asked if he had any questions and if he was ready for disciplinary procedures to begin. He said he had no questions. He was ready.

She then cuffed and locked his wrists to the sides of the table, his ankles to the stirrups. She moved some kind of medical-looking machine near the exam table. "In your case, our client has contracted for an enhanced experience. Most men find corporal punishment more effective when it is carried out immediately after ejaculation. This machine will help with that."

The Butler

From an envelope clipped to his file, she took out a key that unlocked his chastity cage. He noticed he could see the top of her bra through her neckline as she leaned over him. His newly freed penis came to an immediate erection. She put a condom on it and applied some lubricant. Then she turned on the machine and placed its tube over the head of his erection. His prick slid into the tube and the machine began pumping. It was only minutes before the first of two orgasms was brought on by the action of the mechanism.

While the machine worked, the nurse attached a heart monitor leading to his chest and side. After shutting down the pump, she cleaned his genitals and used a razor to shave his pubic hair. "Please don't move. I don't want to cut you." He lay back and stared at the ceiling.

From a tray of bright metal rings and parts, she selected a ring that snugly fit his cock and balls. Then she chose a cock cage from the tray and fitted it on him. Between the two, she used a special tool to screw them together. "There now, that should not come off." She pulled on the cage and inspected the fit. "This cage has small ridges that prevent the penis skin from backing out. They may cause some minor irritation at first, but you will get used to it."

He sat up. "I'm leaving with this on?"

"Yes, it's in the contract you signed. See here, 'surgical steel, ball trap style chastity device with anti-pullout teeth.' I am quite certain this will not come off without this key. It is easy to keep clean. You can see the bars of the cage allow for good air circulation, and the steel barrier at the tip prevents undue stimulation. It is one of the best we have. I hope you will be pleased with it."

He was ready to continue with a chastity device to prevent masturbation, but he had not thought about hard metal. His plastic cage was now cold steel. It felt, somehow, more permanent, inescapable, unforgiving.

He stood when she released him from the exam table. She locked the ankle cuffs together with a short-chain. She locked his wrist cuffs together in front and used a short chain to lock them to his ankle cuffs. "Wait here. From now on, do not speak unless asked! Answer all questions with yes, ma'am, or no ma'am. Do you understand?"

This he was ready for. It had been emphasized in the instructions and in the orientation video. "Yes, Ma'am." She led him to the toilet a second time and waited. When he was done, she had him bend over. She used antiseptic wipes to clean his anus and his cage.

Their shuffling march down the hall was slowed by the short-chain between his ankles. Another woman and the receptionist looked up from the nurses' station. The receptionist made a comment he couldn't hear. The other laughed and turned to watch. The backside of his gown was flapping open for all to see. He tried to hold it closed with his elbows.

They entered an office room with a large desk. He waited, standing in front of the desk, his nurse holding his arm. A woman came in. She was tall and very fit. Jim could tell because the dark leotard and tights revealed the shape of her body inside her open lab coat. Nurse Lanette handed Jim's file to her.

The woman in the lab coat sat behind the desk. "I have reviewed your file, Mr. O'Neall. You are here as a consequence of your voyeurism over a period of months. Is that correct, Mr. O'Neall?

"Um, yes Ma'am."

"Are you now prepared to accept responsibility for your crime of voyeurism and unacceptable masturbation? Are you ready to receive appropriate punishment for lascivious and offensive acts as defined in this contract?

He hesitated and nodded.

Speak clearly, Mr. O'Neall."

"Yes, Ma'am."

"Our client has contracted for a level seven paddling on bare buttocks with disciplinary enhancements.

And secondary punishment for lascivious masturbation? Is this your understanding as well?"

She paused and looked up. "Yes, Ma'am."

"And you have agreed to these punishments as a consequence of your lewd behavior?"

"Yes, Ma'am."

"Very good. My name is Mistress Jacobs. I am quite prepared to carry out our part of the contract. Do you understand a level seven paddling is a severe punishment? It will leave significant bruising, contusions, and marks?"

"Um, yes, Ma'am." The video he watched earlier had several warnings about bruising. He thought he understood what they meant by this talk about bruises. Sometimes Miss Kendall left bruises with her hairbrush. He had learned to treasure them. They rarely lasted three days.

"I see you have signed all the release forms and the contract. Nurse, please take the delinquent into the operating theater and prepare him. I shall join you shortly."

They went through a side door into a large square room. There were cabinets on three sides and a big round light hanging from the ceiling. The far wall was entirely mirrored floor to ceiling. In the middle of the room, there was a padded bench of sorts with three levels. Jim hesitated.

"Don't cause any trouble now. You have done so well." Nurse Lanette whispered. She unlocked his chains. "Knees here. Elbows here."

Jim compiled. His wrists and ankles were locked to the blocks. A thick strap cinched tightly across the small of his back, held him down. Straps behind his knees made the movement of his hips impossible. She adjusted the ceiling light to focus on his backside. A screen embedded in the bench between his arms brightened. He saw his naked bottom very clearly, surrounded by the open gown he still wore. The camera must be in the light, he thought.

"You will be able to watch your own punishment. Isn't that great? They used to have to watch in the mirror. I think this is a great improvement." He didn't answer. Her enthusiasm was disconcerting. He was becoming concerned.

The nurse plugged his heart leads into a monitor at his side. She added a sensor to his finger. Then she adjusted a camera low on the floor in front of him. Soon he could see his face on a second screen.

In the monitor he watched the nurse wipe his bottom and legs with antiseptic. It felt cold as the alcohol evaporated. Then she massaged lotion into his skin. "For resilience," she said, "the moisturizer helps the skin tolerate sustained abuse without breaking down."

She opened the cabinet in front of him to reveal a large television. It showed the entire room. He was the central figure bound and ready. He wondered if the camera was behind the mirror. In the picture of the big monitor he could see the heart monitor next to him. It said Pulse 116. A bit high, he thought. Oxygen OK at 98.

Nurse Lanette put her hand on his back. She leaned close to his ear. "We are all ready. Soon it will be over. I'll be right over there, don't worry. If there is any problem, I will pause the proceedings. Just remember to breathe." She sat down behind a little desk in the corner. They waited silently. Jim's pulse came down to 88. Still high, he thought, but better.

It seemed like a long time, just waiting. Jim began to wonder what else might be on the other side of the mirror. Were people watching him? He tried adjusting his hips so there was less pressure on his new cage. There was little he could do. He looked over at the nurse. She smiled, "It will be alright, Mr. O'Neall. Mistress Jacobs is good at her job. Just remember to breathe. Don't worry. Disciplinary punishments like this don't take long. Just relax."

The woman he met in the office, Mistress Jacobs, came in. She went to a cabinet on his left. He saw her select a long wooden paddle from a collection of paddles and straps. "Are we ready to begin?"

The Butler

Mistress Jacobs was standing behind him, holding the paddle against his naked bottom. He looked up at the television. He could see rows of holes drilled into the polished wood.

From her corner, the nurse answered, "Everything looks good. Pulse regular, blood oxygen normal."

"Excellent. Mr. O'Neall, we are recording your paddling for our client's review and approval. Our work carries a full warranty. If the client is dissatisfied or if you, the delinquent, question the severity of this correction, we offer a complete do-over to ensure good results."

Jim put his head down. He took a breath. "So, are you ready, Mr. O'Neall? You know once we begin there is no turning back. Feel free to shout, complain, and beg all you want. No one can hear and no one will come to your aid. There will be no mercy; your punishment will be completed. This is your last chance to opt-out. Shall we begin, Mr. O'Neall?

"Yes, Ma'am." His voice had more confidence than he. He saw his pulse rise. He took a breath. Mistress Jacobs was to his left.

"Please say your full name for the video."

"James William O'Neall."

"And what punishment are you here to receive for your delinquency?"

"I am here for a level seven paddling."

"And I am just the woman to deliver it." With that, she landed the first of ten hard strokes. The sound exploded in the room. Jim could hardly believe how much it hurt. He stopped breathing with the third. By the seventh, he was certain he could not survive. At ten she stopped.

"Oh my God," he screamed. His mind was spinning. He pulled on his wrist restraints. He twisted around to see her.

"Mr. O'Neall, do I have your full attention now?"

He didn't answer right away. She hit him again three times. He shouted, "Fuck! Yes, Ma'am."

Mr. O'Neall, I won't tolerate swearing. One more outburst like that and you will be punished for it. Do you understand?"

"Yes, Ma'am."
"Mr. O'Neall, you have been charged with the crime of voyeurism and you have pleaded guilty to this crime. Is that correct, Mr. O'Neall?"

"Yes, Ma'am."

She hit him again, "Louder, Mr. O'Neall."

"Yes, Ma'am!"

"Good. You have also been charged with the crime of masturbating without permission. Are you guilty of this crime, Mr. O'Neall?" She tapped the paddle on his shoulders.

"Yes, Ma'am."

In the mirror wall to his right, he saw her pull back. He arched his back, struggling to escape that paddle. He looked down at the monitor and watched in horror at the distortion of his buttocks. The paddle went right through him. He couldn't breathe.

"Are you sorry for your crimes, Mr. O'Neall?"

He inhaled deeply. "Yes, Ma'am!"

"Mr. O'Neall, do you need to be punished for your crimes?"

Another deep breath, "Yes, Ma'am."

"Very good. After each stroke, you will apologize for your misdeeds and ask politely for the next one. 'I'm sorry,' followed by 'May I have another?' Do you understand, Mr. O'Neall?"

"Yes, Ma'am." As he got the Ma'am out of his mouth, the sound of the paddle on flesh exploded. "Oh God, I'm sorry. May I have another?"

As the beating continued, his apologies melted into tears. When he stopped asking for another, the strokes began falling fast and hard. She worked both sides of his butt cheeks focusing on one for several strokes, then the other. The room filled with the sound of his punishment and his cries: he begging her to stop, the paddle relentlessly striking flesh. He pulled on his bindings as hard as he could. He cried out.

"Please stop, please stop, please stop, please..." Jim kept repeating. With every stroke, his shoulders jerked up, but the belt across his lower back held him in place. There was no avoiding her paddle. In the monitor, he saw it land over and over. She worked on the back of his thighs. He started sobbing. Tears flowed.

"You beg for mercy, but did you have any mercy as you abused your position in our client's household? What is your crime, Mr. O'Neall?" She prodded his back with the paddle.

Between heavy sobs he said, "I... looked... at her... underwear."

"Voyeurism is a serious offense. Do you agree?"

"Yes, Ma'am. Please Ma'am." He continued begging between sobs.

She cut him off, "So now, in the midst of receiving just a reward, you are sorry for abusing your trusted position?

The Butler

"Yes, I am sorry. Please, Ma'am."

"So, now might we go back to apologizing and asking for another?"

"Oh my God, Ma'am. Please, Ma'am. Please "

"I take that for a yes. I want you to look directly into the camera in front of you and apologize to our client for your behavior."

"Yes, Ma'am. Jennifer, I apologize for betraying your trust in me.

"Now ask for another."

"Please Ma'am, No!"

"I take that to be a request for another stroke." With that she delivered and he howled. "Your apology to our client?"

"Jennifer, I apologize for betraying your trust in me."

"And your request?"

"Please, Ma'am. Owww! Fuck!"

"Mister O'Neall, what did I say about using that term?"

Between sobs, he got out, "I... would... be... punished."

"Exactly. Mr. O'Neall. Nurse Lanette, would you be so kind as to wash Mr. O'Neall's mouth out with soap?"

The nurse brought a bowl of water from her desk in which a bar of Ivory soap had been softening. Mistress Jacobs pulled his head back by his hair and Nurse Lanette pressed the softened bar of soap against his closed lips. "Open up, Mr. O'Neall! This won't hurt. I'll be careful." The awful taste of the soap made him gag. Nurse Lanette made sure to rub the bar against all his teeth and his tongue, soap lather filled his mouth. He couldn't get it off his tongue. She rubbed his face with it.

"There now, Mr. O'Neall, we can now begin again with your final thirty-six. I trust we will have no more use of that word."

Thirty-six strokes later, thirty-six apologies later, Miss Jacob's announced, "I believe we have dealt with the offence of voyeurism sufficiently.

"Thank you, Ma'am." He let out a long breath and relaxed a little, spitting soap into the towel.

"But your offensive behavior also included masturbation while imagining our client in her underwear. I believe we have yet to deal effectively with that obnoxious and vulgar behavior. Which hand do you use to masturbate, Mr. O'Neall?"

Jim didn't answer right away. She came round to the front, holding the paddle before him. Jim could see his blood on it

"Your chart says you use your left hand to masturbate. Is that true, Mr. O'Neall?"

"Yes, left hand."

"I think we should deal with your repulsive behavior by using the tawes on your offensive left hand, rather than continuing paddling on your backside, don't you agree, Mr. O'Neall?"

He didn't answer right away, he didn't understand her question. "Do we need to continue with this paddle on your backside, Mr. O'Neall?"

"No, Ma'am!" He shouted as loudly as he could.

"Shall we deal with your repulsive behavior, unacceptable masturbation with tawes, Mr. O'Neall?"

"Yes, Ma'am." Jim was completely defeated. The soap made it difficult to speak clearly. He tried to push it out of his mouth. He was drooling uncontrollably into a towel the nurse put there for the purpose.
The paddle was exchanged for a leather strap with two tails. Mistress Jacobs returned to stand in front of him. "Mr. O'Neall, please extend your left hand, palm up. Yes, just like that." The restraints allowed

him to offer his hand, resting on the bench. She waited a moment, as if considering the situation.

"Now, I might have thought twelve strokes appropriate severe correction for masturbating in this ugly manner, but you have agreed to wear a chastity device. So perhaps we can reduce the punishment in half. What do you say to that, Mr. O'Neall?"

"Yes Ma'am. Thank you "Ma'am."

"So, you hereby agree to six strokes with the tawes to your left hand as punishment for masturbating without consent?"

"Yes, Ma'am. I'm sorry Ma'am."

"You will be sorry young man. Please count each stroke and thank me for it. Do you understand?"

"Yes, Ma'am. Thank you, Ma'am." With that, she brought the leather down hard across his outstretched hand. He howled, "Oh My God!" He pulled his hand back. She waited for him to say "One, thank you." And extended his hand again. Two through six brought the same reaction.

"Your level seven correction is now complete unless you want more, Mr. O'Neall. Do you want another six?"

He was quick to shout, "No Ma'am. Thank you, Ma'am. I have had enough, Ma'am. Please, Ma'am. No more, Ma'am. Please, Ma'am."

The nurse was at his side. "It's OK, Mr. O'Neall. Your punishment is over. That didn't take long. I just have to give some first aid before I get you down from there." She stroked his head. "See, I told you Mistress Jacobs is good at her job. I almost had to pause the proceedings because you were holding your breath. But then she had you sobbing and your oxygen saturation went right back up."

The nurse wiped his face with another towel. She put antiseptic cream on areas where his buttocks were abraded and two large bandages on places where the skin had broken open. She cleaned up the blood. Detaching him from the restraints, she said his disciplinary session was complete. He could use the sink in the room to rinse the soap out of his mouth, "You may use the towel to wipe out your mouth."

She led him to an adjacent room. The basket with his clothes was on the table. "You may dress, James. And please drink some of this water. Punishments are dehydrating. We are almost done."

"Why did you soap my mouth like that? It's awful."

"Mr. O'Neall, you brought that on yourself when you continued to swear. You were warned. It's alright. It happens often enough that I always prepare a bowl of water with soap in it. Boys shouldn't swear in our presence. We understand prayer. Phrases like 'Oh God' might be religious, so we tolerate them. But we find words like the one you used to be intolerable."

"That was horrible, it is horrible. I can't get it out of my mouth."

"Yes, yes, Mr. O'Neall." She put her arm around his shoulder. "I'm sure you will survive this too. When you get home, brush your teeth with plenty of water! It will help." She left him to get dressed.

He touched his bottom. It was hard and uneven. The back of his legs just hurt. No matter how much he wiped out his mouth, he couldn't get rid of the soap. His lips and gums were raw. He dressed slowly. He kept his left hand flat against his chest as much as he could. Without thinking, he sat to put on his socks and shoes. It was agony. He groaned. The door opened.

"Mr. O'Neall! Very few choose to sit down after severe corrections! I am impressed." The receptionist came in carrying the tray with his wallet, phone, and keys. "Delinquents usually stand while I do the exit interview. There is nothing in the manual that says you must stand, so you may remain seated."

Jim shifted in the wooden chair. There was no comfort to be found, but he stayed where he was because she said she was impressed.

"It appears you must have used some bad words, Mr. O'Neall. I can see the soap on your face. I thought you were more of a gentleman than that. I trust the soap cured you of swearing while here?"

"It was awful."

"There, there, Mr. O'Neall. Big boys learn to accept the consequences of their actions."

"I have a few questions for you. Did the overall experience meet your expectations?"

"It went way beyond any expectation I had."

"Oh, how so?"

"It was terrifying. It hurt way more than you can imagine."

"Oh, Mr. O'Neall, I work here. I do the exit interviews. I have a good idea about the level of pain involved. Wait until you come back for judicial punishment!"

"I'm never coming back."

"That is so good to hear, Mr. O'Neall. It means we provided just the right correction for you. May I assume that you feel Mistress Jacobs did her job well?"

"Oh my God. I never want to meet that woman again."

The receptionist laughed. "Mr. O'Neall, Mistress Jacobs is a delightful person. I am sure you would like her if you got to know her."

"She did her job. That's all I want to know about her."

How were our greetings and preparation? Did you feel adequately prepared for your punishment session?"

"You and Nurse Lanette were both very kind and helpful. Without Nurse Lanette, I don't think I would have made it through."

"If you send a thank-you note, it will go to Nurse Lanette's personnel file. We don't get many of those from delinquents. We frequently receive them from clients. One last thing, Mr. O'Neall, the new chastity cage you have on needs to be checked weekly for next month. Our client suggested Thursdays after work would be good for you. Say 7:15?"

"Just to check the cock cage?"

"No more corrections, unless you want it. Sometimes delinquents become clients who contract for themselves. Mistress Jacobs does private sessions. She is one of our best. Here is a brochure on our many services. So, Thursday evening at 7:15?"

"Yes Ma'am."

Nurse Lanette escorted him to his car and handed him the water bottle. He had some difficulty getting in. His back was stiff. She waved as she went back to the building. He started his car. It was after 2:00.

He drove home on city streets, up Cicero Avenue. His whole body ached. His neck stiffened up on his drive. The seat warmer was helpful. After he parked, he stayed in the car for another twenty minutes drinking the water. It tasted like soap; it burned his mouth. He could feel it in his throat. Getting out of the car was not easy. He took the elevator up.

Exhausted, he lay face down on his bed and went to sleep. He woke up when Jennifer came home that evening. She knocked at his door. He got up to open it.

"Poor dear, you look miserable. Was it difficult for you?"

"In a word, yes."

"They said you might be uncomfortable for a couple of days. That's why I asked for Friday. You have the weekend to recover. They also said it would be good to rehydrate. I brought you a Propel liter for you." He accepted the bottle from her.

"They also said you should not have alcohol or strong painkillers. Only aspirin to reduce swelling. Here is a bottle of 81mg. I brought home a 10 lb. bag of ice. When you are ready, they recommended an ice water sitz bath to promote healing."

"That does not sound like fun." He stood in the doorway holding the water bottle and the pills.
"It will be good for you. They said ice this evening, heat later."

"Jennifer, I am sorry for what I did. I have been punished enough. I don't want to sit in ice."

"James, I am concerned about you. I want what's best for you and for me. If ice will get you back to normal quicker, then we should do it."

The firmness of her voice drew a reluctant assent to an ice bath. He sat on his bed. His back hurt. She got 10 lbs. of ice cubes from the freezer and dumped them in his tub along with a couple of inches of cold water. She told him to undress and get in. She left his room.

The bruising he saw in the mirror was way more extensive than he imagined. He was deep purple from near the top of his butt to halfway down his thighs. Jennifer never left bruising like that. He gently peeled the bandages from his skin and got into the tub. Lowering himself into ice water was excruciating. He lifted himself above the water every few minutes. His penis shriveled in its cage. He thought his scrotum might have frozen to its steel ring.

Twenty minutes later, he got out and inspected his bottom some more. The places he bled were not as purple as the rest. After the ice bath, the bleeding stopped and the bruising was more varied. He could see the full outline of the paddle in a couple of places on his thigh. There were small round marks left by the holes in the paddle everywhere.
He put on his robe and went back out to the kitchen. He made himself a sandwich, but he couldn't taste it. He ate only half. "Jennifer, I'm going to bed," he called out.

She was watching the evening news. "Tomorrow morning, then. Have a good sleep."

He was awake before his alarm went off. The new chastity cage was more comfortable. His back hurt like he had been lifting way too much weight. He had trouble bending. He felt his bottom. It was still hard and uneven, but not as painful. The soap was making its way through his digestive tract. He could tell because his stomach gurgled. The taste of the soap lingered. He got up, brushed his teeth again, and dressed. Jennifer worked most Saturdays. He did not. He went to make coffee.

She smiled when he gave her the mug. "Back to normal, I see. That is good. Very good. Did the bath help?"

"I think it did. Thank you for the ice."

"I believe your instructions are to take another ice bath this morning. There is more ice in the freezer. Then, I purchased a new electric heat pad. It is on the counter over there."

He was silent. Finally, he said "OK." He saw only her blue eyes.

"James, we need to talk about the past week and where we go from here. I have cancelled my engagements for this evening. Perhaps you might have dinner ready at 7:00 for the two of us?"

He made a simple dinner of roast chicken and vegetables. He chilled a California Chardonnay from her wine collection for her to have with it. They ate together. He cleared the table and loaded the dishwasher. It was difficult to lean over to fill the bottom rack. She invited him into the television room. "I need to review the video report they sent. I'd like us to do it together."

He had not thought about the video. They said they would send a video to her. But he didn't imagine actually watching it. He knew he had lost it. He cried, and begged, and lost all dignity in the process. He was suddenly not sure he wanted her to see his breakdown. "Are you sure you want to watch this?"

"James, I have to sign off on your punishment. Otherwise, they will have to do it all over. It's in the contract."

She sat on the sofa; he on three cushions at her feet. The video started with him being led into the chamber and strapped down. "The nurse looks gentle."

"She was wonderful. Without her, I would not have survived."

"That's good. She is doing a thorough job!" A picture in the picture popped up in one corner showing a close up of Jim's butt, then another of his face. The nurse rubbed lotion on the bottom of the picture. Jim heard her say it was "for resilience."

"I'm not sure if that worked. My butt doesn't feel resilient today."

"Oh, I'm glad your sense of humor is back." Jennifer smiled. He looked up at her; he smiled back.

They watched Mistress Jacobs come into the room. Her heels clicked on the floor. They heard Jim's apology and request for another melt into cries and terror. For a while, there was the near-constant sound of the paddle striking flesh. His face twisted in pain. He begged and pleaded. Finally, he was sobbing. The close-up of his face showed the tears streaming.

Jennifer put her hand on Jim's head. With each of his thirty-six apologies after the mouth soaping, Jennifer responded, "You are forgiven." But the howl from Jim in the video drowns out her forgiveness. Soap foam covered his face. He drooled uncontrollably. He screamed his apologies. No dignity remaining, he looked broken.

Jim looked up at Jennifer. Her eyes were on the screen. Jim's punishment had her complete attention.

The closing six with the tawes came as a denouement, a falling action separate from the flurry of sound. But the way his shoulders strained and his exclamations after each stroke confirmed the power of each impact. Jennifer shifted in her seat. Each time the horrible leather strap landed; her fingers on his head tensed. Jim watched as he willingly extended his own hand six times.

Jennifer said, "My, that was something! I think we can safely say that they kept their side of the contract." She stroked his head. He sat quietly staring at the blank screen, her hand on his head.

"Yes..."

Jennifer seemed focused. "That was intense. Let's watch it again."

The second time through his punishment, Jim was able to watch Mistress Jacobs. He had not seen her take off her lab coat after coming into the room. He watched her hang it up on a hook by the door. She moved with the grace of an athlete. He was not aware of the black gloves she wore. He had not known she kicked off her heels and knelt to tie on athletic shoes. Her body was slender, strong, confident. Dark hair framed her face. For the rest of his life, Mistress Jacobs appeared in his dreams.

She wielded the paddle with grace, effortlessly stepping into each stroke, driving it home, following through, turning, ready for the next. She concentrated on her target, on his reaction, on her purpose. When he started holding his breath, she increased the power of her strokes going lower on his thighs. He screamed and started crying; wailing loudly as if to cover up the sound of the paddle. She went back to a faster paced beating of his backside. Watching, Jim was mesmerized, by the recording of his own punishment.

Together, they watched the video three times. Jim found it a bit disconcerting that Jennifer seemed to enjoy it so much. He looked up and saw her radiant, eyes wide, mouth open, fully attentive to the beating he received. But she repeated his forgiveness and he was happy. Sunday afternoon he wrote a letter to MCDS.

To the staff of MCCS, thank you.

Cynthia and Nurse Lanette made my arrival and intake more than pleasant. They explained everything in the most friendly manner. They were both very kind. I really felt no fear until Nurse Lanette, took me into the operating room. Her encouragement got me past that hump. Without Nurse Lanette I am not sure I would have been able to go through with my punishment and reap its reward.

Mistress Jacobs was perfect. She was all business. Her confident demeanor matched her expertise and skill. From the moment I met her, I was both intimidated and certain of her capabilities. My punishment at her hands was severe. There was no question about that. Miss Kendall seems well satisfied and I have no desire to return for more. But were I ever to return, I should request Mistress Jacobs.

The person I most want to thank is Miss Lake, our consultant. Without her intervention, I fear I would be homeless today. She clarified my offense and defined the consequence clearly. Miss Kendall was pleased and that made me say it was all worth it.

In short, thank you for a job well done.

Sincerely,

James O'Neall

He folded his letter and took it with him for his appointment to have his cage checked. He gave his letter to the receptionist. Neither Cynthia nor Nurse Lanette worked evenings. Nurse Rachel took care of him. He didn't have to strip naked, just his pants. She checked him over and announced his cage was clean. She also commented on his bruises. She said they were healing well. "You are good to go. We will see you in a week."

The following Sunday morning, Jennifer knocked on his door. They sat across from each other at the dining room table. She started by asking how he was doing. He replied that his backside was still healing, but he felt very good about how things were going.

"You must have given the Midway organization a really good letter. I have received comments from several of the staff, including the woman who paddled you. Apparently, they don't get many thank you letters from people they have disciplined."
"Yeah, I wrote a short note. They did their job, and I still live here."

"About that. We need to talk."

"OK." Suddenly, he was concerned.

"You have a new chastity cage. They check it three more times. That is a month and a week with your genitals caged. I am concerned about what will happen next month. Do we go back to the way it was? I am not certain I am ready to have to worry about your, um, fetish."

"I assure you; you have nothing to fear from me. I have learned my lesson."

"I'm sure you mean what you say..."

"I am prepared to wear this thing until you have confidence in me again. I want to stay here."

"Oh, I am so glad to hear that. I am relieved. I was concerned that we might have a crisis coming, but the crisis averted!" Her eyes were shown. She was all smiles. He lived for her smile.

For three more Thursday evenings, he went back, waiting to park until the last minute. The nurse complimented him on the way he kept himself clean. "Baths helped," he said. The irritation brought on by the anti-pullout teeth subsided. He was becoming acclimated to wearing his chastity device. Sometimes he even forgot it was there.

In his last visit to Midway Corrections, the nurse talked about longer-term use of the cage. She suggested that some men find it more comfortable to use a piercing in the penis to secure the tube rather than, or as a supplement to the ball trap. She gave him a brochure. "Of course, Mr. O'Neall, if you choose this option, we would be pleased to handle all the necessary preparations right here in this office."

On his way out, Mistress Jacobs stopped him in the hall. "Mr. O'Neall, I understand this may be your last visit with us. I wanted to let you know I thoroughly enjoyed our time together. Thank you for choosing us."

"You enjoyed?"

"Oh yes. I don't always get feedback from the people I discipline. Your session was memorable. The way you vocalized and carried on made you a real joy to paddle. Then your note was an unexpected pleasure. You may come back anytime. I do so love punishing you."

"Thanks, Mistress Jacobs, don't be offended when I say that I sincerely hope we never meet again. Don't get me wrong, I think about you often. You made a great first impression. It has taken me weeks to get over it."

She laughed. "And here I was hoping you would be back for more. I'm glad to hear that you think of me. I will remember you. Goodbye Mr. O'Neall. I'm off to do a delicious, very severe, level nine caning. Poor sot, it will be his third session. You'd think he would have learned his lesson as well as you have." She gave him a hug. He left.

Emma J. Nobis

CHAPTER THREE

The next few years were very happy ones for him. His job was meaningless, his great passion for Miss Kendall's home. She set goals for his health, sending him to a personal trainer three evenings a week. He took additional cooking classes, especially baking and pastry. His whole life revolved around hers. Every evening he looked forward to the moment she walked through the door.

He even catered a dinner party for seven of her guests. The reviews were good. She was pleased. She complimented him on the way he kept her underwear clean and folded. "Much better than machine washing." Her compliments meant everything to him. Still conscious of the need to give her space at home, he did not dote. Instead, he greeted her and retired to the kitchen, laundry, or health club.

She put him over her knee whenever he needed it. But he needed it less often. There was a reason. Six months after his paddling, Jim broached the subject of being allowed some time out of chastity, a holiday of sorts. "Are you planning on going somewhere?" she asked.

"No, but I thought we should discuss when we might let me go free for a limited time."

"Ah James, you have been so attentive these past few months, and I have felt so free around you. You wouldn't want to change that, would you?"
"Of course not, Ma'am." He had taken to responding to her questions that way. "I only thought maybe there could be an alternative."

"Are you finding your little cage frustrating? It has the opposite effect on me. I find it empowering."

"I just thought."

"Yes, I understand James. Miss Lake warned me when we got into this contract that someday you would beg to be free. She offered an alternative plan."

"Yes, Ma'am?"

"She said they have a release option for long-term chastity wearers. You and I decide upon an appropriate cost for release and they take care of it all."

"I don't understand."

"To put it bluntly, you remember the enhanced option before your paddling? We simply agree on the cost for release. They drain your balls before applying the cost - some form of corporal punishment, I expect."

"Let me think about that."

"Certainly James."

Not long after, they decided the cost would be six English style cane strokes: "six of the best." Mistress Jacobs was very happy to see him again. She told him she didn't get to use the cane nearly as often as she liked. She enjoyed caning him. He never failed to howl and complain.

He was not strapped down for his caning. After the nurse unhooked him from the machine, he would kneel, head to floor until Mistress Jacobs entered.

At her instruction, he stood and bent over the exam table, backside bare. The nurse used her phone to make a recording. Mistress Jacob took her time between strokes. This was not punishment, only the cost of release. She acted as if this was fun, even enjoyable. James, somehow, never got past the absolute agony of each stroke. He wished she would just get it over with. Six quick strokes must be better than having to wait for the inevitable wave of searing pain each time.

Even so, Jennifer seemed to believe that enhanced caning was a reward for good behavior. Every few months, Jennifer would announce his reward and then review, with him, the video recording of the caning. She would rub his head while they watched his face contort with each stroke. To James, the video seemed like his gift to her. The smile watching it was a reward for him.

A year later, things began to change. Jennifer thought it would be good for him to learn some personal self-defense. It might give him self-confidence. They decided to unlock him on Sundays so he could participate in martial arts classes. She set the key out for him as if she had a guest with her on Sunday morning. Sunday afternoon after class, he locked himself back in the cage. He dropped the key into a lockbox he purchased for that purpose. It had a slot on top. He enjoyed her confidence in him. He kept his promise - no masturbation - because she expected it of him.

Sundays were all on the honor system, but once in a while on Monday morning, she checked to be sure he was locked up. Unannounced, she would put her hand on his pants, feeling for the cage. "Very good, James," she would say. Her bright eyes never failed to make him feel proud and happy.

With major litigation at hand, Jennifer spent long hours at her office, often including evenings and weekends. Jim thought she might like dinner at work. He prepared her favorite fire-roasted vegetables with seared ahi tuna. He delivered it to her office. He cut it all into bite-size pieces so she could use chopsticks even though it wasn't Asian. He used a balsamic reduction sauce with toasted sesame seeds.

She was surrounded by files. Two junior associates scurried in and out of her office. She said, "Why thank you, James?" Her smile was all he could ask for. He took to delivering dinner whenever she worked late and responded "yes" to his text query.

As the lead attorney in an international patent infringement case, she worked hard. She brought the plaintiff corporation to her firm. She acted as outside counsel for the client's company. She would argue in the Federal Court and before the World Trade Organization. This one case could make her a full partner. He wanted to be supportive in every way possible.

He took care of her life, freeing her to work on her project. She let him manage everything. He managed her accounts, paying her bills and writing checks. She signed them when she came home. He sent them out the next day. That's how he learned how much Midway Correction charged for one of his visits. Only then did he realize what she spent on him. To pay that much for his "release" from chastity meant a lot.

He hated the cane but loved kneeling before Mistress Jacobs. He hated his genitals locked up, but loved serving Miss Kendall. He loved the orgasm but hated the machine the nurse used to make it happen. His life was full of love and contradictions. Now he knew its value.

"Thank you for that," he told her as she signed the Midway Corrections check.

"No problem," she responded, handing the check back to him. "You are worth every penny." He wanted to hug her, but that wasn't their relationship. Her blue eyes glowed. He leaned over the table to put the check in the envelope he had prepared. She patted him on the head and scratched behind his ear. He bent his head toward her. "Good boy."

He sat down. "I have been a little curious. When I deliver dinner to you at your office, who do you tell others I am?"

"Yes, it is a bit odd, isn't it? I mean 'roommate' gives the wrong impression and 'friend' doesn't cut it."

"I've been thinking about this."

"And you have a suggestion?"

"What about Butler?"

"Really? Butler?"

"In organizing your bills and filing your receipts I have become aware of how much I cost. I was under the complete misapprehension that I was paying my way with what I contributed. So, I began wondering what I am to you. Butler seemed the best term I could come up with. I would hate housekeepers."

"If you like butler, then butler it is." She smiled. He liked her smile. "Would my butler like an over the knee spanking to seal the deal before I go back to the office?"

"Yes Ma'am, thank you, Ma'am."

"Alright James. Go get my grandmother's hairbrush."

He felt very good about his new title. When she made a full partner, they moved to a large home in Kenilworth, north of Chicago. He stopped working outside her home and became her full-time butler. She was Miss Kendall to him, he James to her. He drove her to appointments when she asked. She rode in the back seat. He even bought a hat for that purpose. He did so like hearing, "Home, James."

"Very good, Ma'am," his responded.

She hired a maid to help with the housework. He supervised the maid and the gardeners and all the contractors. He managed her affairs, seeing to it that everything in her life outside her office was graceful and effortless. Even with the housekeeper present, he kept the task of hand-washing Miss Kendall's lingerie as his own. He was confident that no one could do it better.

She made a change in the contract with Midway Correction and Domination Services. Mistress Jacobs and a nurse assistant made a monthly house call to their home in Kenilworth. Jennifer enjoyed watching the six strokes in person. She made herself available when she was in town. If not, the nurse recorded the caning and sent it directly to her phone. It was important to him that she received the record of his suffering.

His self-defense classes proved useful. She had a problem with a particular Saturday evening 'gentleman caller.' There was a disagreement about her level of commitment to the relationship. He wanted exclusivity. She ordered her guest to leave. He refused. She felt threatened. They were in the living room. She pushed the button to summon James. He was in the home gym working out.

When he entered the room, he sized up the situation and stepped in between Miss Kendall and the visitor. While the man was bigger than him, James's new confidence in his own fighting ability caused the visitor to back down, pick up his coat and leave. "Thank you, James. I am so glad you were here." He made it a point to be available anytime he knew she was going to have a visitor. Her safety became his responsibility. As in everything else, he carried out his new role as invisibly as possible.

Increasingly, as an international contract law attorney, Jennifer was called out of town and out of the country. In her absence James managed her affairs and kept her house. Ultimately, she gave him the power to sign her checks. When away, Jennifer allowed him more discretion in wearing his chastity cage. He had the key. But it was now so much a part of his life, he only took it off for workouts. Besides, he knew what Miss Kendall desired of him.

Jim never thought about the last time he had sex or even masturbated on his own. His only thought was Miss Kendall, her needs, and her concerns. Together they decided a Prince Albert piercing would make his chastity easier to manage. When she was in town, she always kept his key.

The threat of Brexit caused disruption in the EU offices of her London-based firm. The senior partners decided to open new offices in Dublin and Strasbourg as a hedge against the fallout from a potential "no deal" British exit from the EU. They asked Jennifer to head the Strasbourg office startup. It was a great opportunity. It could lead to a senior partnership.

So, it happened, James accompanied Miss Kendall to Strasbourg. He chauffeured her to and from the office each day and maintained her home there. She entertained frequently. They hired a sous chef, but James set the menu, managed the kitchen, and served dinner. He often stood by the kitchen door as guests ate and conversed. He watched for her smile.

It was James who suggested that Miss Kendal herself provide the cost for his reward and release. She was only too happy to oblige. He used the machine on himself and Miss Kendall caned him. Six strokes, always six strokes, the cost of release. He suffered for her. But she was his life's great purpose. He could not recall the last time he felt depressed. She would rub his head after the sixth strike. He waited in position, bent over the side chair in her room, for that caress.

When, at 93, he suffered a stroke, she took care of him. "I'm so glad I chose you all those years ago." Breaking her own rule of fifty years, she leaned in and kissed him. They were quiet together, his hand in hers. She smiled. He always liked her smile. He spoke his final words to her.

Jennifer was at his bedside when her butler died. "Complications following his stroke." Memories of a life well lived flooded the room as she processed his final words. Back 40 years ago, when she was not yet 30, she posted her ad on Craigslist.

He was not the first to answer that ad. He was not the first she tried as a roommate. When she first signed on as a junior associate in her law firm, she shared an apartment with another young attorney. Both were beginning their career, but the other woman wanted to party instead of building her resume.

That first roommate did not last long at the firm nor in her apartment. Over the next four years, there was a succession of three other young attorneys, none of whom were as driven as she.

She had enough powerful men in her life. She could bring one home anytime she wanted. She decided she did not want to live with someone full of himself.

She began looking for someone she could shape into the person with whom she could live.

The first one she chose, who answered her Craigslist ad, was talkative. The bigger problem was, after a couple of months, he began to see her as a potential lover even though she clearly stated otherwise. She did not want to have to repel his advances. He was not trainable, he cared only about himself.

The second, she tried was a young woman who had a lot of growing up to do. While compliant, this one proved more needy than useful. She lasted three months.

Then Jim showed up. She knew right away. There was no question. He was the right one. He didn't recognize her, but she met him once before. He had been a client of one of her associates. She recognized him, yet, over the decades, he never seemed to recollect having met her.

In high school, Jennifer was sexually active. Actually, that may be an understatement. Better put, Jennifer explored as fully as possible her sexual identity while in high school. As soon as she came of age in her state, she went beyond boys learning about their own sexuality, to men who knew what they wanted. And she gave them what they wanted. She also learned that they would give back when she asked.

The Butler

In the spring of her senior year in high school, a gentleman admirer gave her an expensive necklace. That set up an exploration of ways she could pay for college as an escort on weekends. Her freshman year at college, Jennifer got really good at sucking dick and earned enough to pay for her first two years.

She advertised on Backpage but found she got a better response, at that time, from an ad on Eros. She was busy most weekends and, with experience, found she could sort out those who would not generously support her. While engaged in the world of sex work, she maintained boundaries with her life as a college student, keeping her identity secret.

In the spring of her sophomore year, she met a client who asked for a spanking. Not a little love taps as a prelude to sex, but a full-out over-the-knee spanking with a wooden hairbrush. Jennifer never looked back. His struggle to stay over her knee while his bottom turned pink, then deep red, then white in spots was as exciting to her as all the sex she ever had.

She signed up to work at a local commercial BDSM dungeon and found her calling. She loved dominating men. And she was good at it. In her junior year, she gave up advertising as an escort and immersed herself in professional domination as "Mistress Agony." Beyond her fascination with the varieties of submission, she enjoyed being with those who would suffer for her, and suffer as they did.

She soaked up the wisdom of the headmistress, working with her as often as she could. That is how she met Jim. He was a client of the headmistress: his preferred session corporal; his preferred instrument the paddle. Jennifer never had a session with him, but she saw him in the dungeon. Once she greeted him at the door in her role as Mistress Agony. He didn't seem to make the connection when they met in her office for the interview. Why would he?

Jennifer graduated from college and law school near the top of her class. More importantly, she graduated debt-free with money in her brokerage account. She snagged an excellent offer from an international law firm. On her income from the law firm, without the debt that burdened so many junior law associates, she could afford a nice apartment in a great neighborhood.

She left sex work behind. With hard work and clarity on her goals, Jennifer began climbing the ladder at the firm. Initially, to manage costs, she shared her apartment with other associates. But each proved difficult. That's when she had the idea that has changed everything. What if she could find a submissive? Could she find a submissive who would share some of the cost of her apartment, help with everyday tasks, and defer authority to her?

When Jim walked through her door to interview, she knew that if her idea was going to work, it would be with him. Already on his third day with her, when he handed her a mug of coffee, her smile was honest. "This is the way it will be," she thought. She could tell he liked her smile.

It didn't take long, just a few weeks, to train him to clean and take care of the apartment for her. She never used an angry word, just her smile. She found he responded to encouraging gestures. His most enthusiastic service was when he thought it was his idea. She directed his thoughts rather than his behavior. The single most important thing to her was respect for her boundaries. And, while his consent to her process of training was never explicit, his unique joy derived from her smile gave her the permission she desired.

A look of disappointment was seldom necessary. When he overslept one day, she thought, at first, she may have overdone her disapproval. [Her Butler part 1] He became sullen and unresponsive. Knowing that his preferred sessions at the dungeon involved impact play, she decided to offer a spanking. It made all the difference. His attitude improved immediately. And a wholly new level of relationship formed.

Jennifer loved spanking Jim. Her grandmother's hairbrush was the perfect implement. She dug it out of a box in her apartment storage area long before he gave her a reason to use it. She waited for the right time and when that time arrived, the hairbrush made its appearance. The story of its use on the women in her family provided the perfect level of connection for him.

With spanking their only act of intimacy, Jennifer and Jim made their home together. It remained her apartment with Jim the renter, but it was more than that. Jim found the purpose for his life in her apartment. His happiness became connected to her wellbeing and her pleasure. For him, an hour cleaning when she wasn't there was an hour close to her. But when she was there, he took pains to be out of the way. Odd how this contradiction made perfect sense to both of them. He fulfilled her expectation of him and his desire to serve.

Jim gave her space to live while taking care of the apartment. He enjoyed doing what he could to make her life easier. No one couldn't ask more submissive questions. His financial contribution was not as great as her former roommates, but he more than made up for it in his willing service to her. While he never explicitly expressed consent to her dominance, he gave his submission without her consent as well. It was their way.

And those spankings! Jennifer revealed in spanking Jim. His delicious squirming aroused her; his timing was uncanny. She might have a particularly difficult day preparing a legal brief, or with an obtuse client or with office politics, and her hairbrush would appear on the chair by the window. It was his sign he was ready or was it he sensed she needed to spank him?

The Butler

He always seemed to know the perfect moment to ask. And for the days leading up to their Sunday morning encounter, that antique hairbrush on her chair evoked, in her, the arousal to come. He offered his bottom. She took advantage of his offering. She delighted in his suffering even as he coveted standing in the corner of her room.

When she made Junior Partner in the firm, they moved to an upper floor condo purchased with her savings. Her investment paid off when later she made a full partner. She used a cash-out mortgage on the condo for her partnership to buy-in. Then, after her second-year distribution, she bought a home in Kenilworth, just north of the city. Jennifer made shrewd choices.

James was one of those shrewd choices. When he lost his job as a warehouse manager, she lowered his rent to something he could afford as a Starbucks barista. He had more time to think up ways to support her, becoming her cook, housemaid, and maintenance man, all in one.

The tranquility of her home life balanced the intensity of her law office. Jim made their home a place of peace. He absolutely never complained to her about anything. He did the shopping and took care of her household. He gave her the receipts and she reimbursed him. It was their way.

Saturday evenings, Jim would vanish. She could bring anyone home with her and there would be no sign of Jim's presence. She wondered if he could hear her lovemaking, but he said nothing. Unless they had a date with her hairbrush, she would not see him on the weekend until Sunday evening.

Often, in contract law, her work involved creating compromise solutions. Bending her client just enough to make the transaction happen, with a profitable result. Until both sides signed, the negotiations were often tense. Like a high-stakes game of chess, she had to plan several responses to the next proposal from the other side. She was good at it, this negotiation phase, and she was promoted to even more intense situations.

Having a peaceful home was a godsend to her. She never felt the conflicts in her personal life others experienced. Because of Jim, Jennifer's life was free of drama. She was able to focus on her clients and their best interests; often understanding their best options better than they did. She developed a reputation for positive outcomes when others could see only a stalemate.

When she discovered Jim going through her underwear drawer, she was a little angry. [Her Butler Part 2] He had violated the implicit boundary between them that made the peace she enjoyed possible. Her first impulse was to end their relationship. But she had invested years in training him. She decided this was an opportunity to take their relationship to a new level. That's when she thought of JoEllen.

The Butler

She knew JoEllen had a great commercial BDSM facility on the south side. It was in an old medical building with a warren of rooms for various themes. Jennifer contacted her and set up a very special session for Jim. Jennifer designed it all. Of course, she knew Jim's history. She knew his appetite for corporal punishment from years before. She engaged three of JoEllen's house dominas to play the parts of the receptionist, nurse, and corporal punishment specialist.

It was JoEllen who came up with the idea of chastity and washing underwear, but Jennifer loved it. Putting the two ideas together, corporal punishment and long-term chastity, was perfect for Jim. His submission was complete; satisfying both to him and to her.

The room in which Jim received his paddling has a wall of two-way mirrors. Behind the mirror wall is a small lounge for the staff. From there they can view sessions and learn from each other. Of course, Jennifer attended and watched Jim's session from behind that mirror. Later, when she was available, she would watch his canings. His suffering pleased her no end. She kept the video of his paddling and sometimes watched it on her smartphone while waiting in airports.

The most difficult part of Jim's punishment scene to produce was the orientation video. Jennifer knew a kink-friendly videographer from her time in the commercial dungeon. She wrote the script and had a graphic artist make a storyboard to go along with it. They filmed the storyboard and the woman who played the receptionist did the voiceover.

All in all, that Friday morning and the four Thursday evenings cost more than fourteen thousand dollars. But it was well worth it. Even the actor who walked out to his car with the help of the nurse was paid. Jennifer scripted Jim's experience from beginning to end. She had given him the gift of an experience he would never forget. And in return, she had the key to his chastity cage.

Locked in chastity, Jim became even more attentive. He was the one who suggested that he might cater to a dinner party for one of her clients. She was concerned, so she set up a dinner with some of her staff. That went so well, she agreed to Jim's plan.

Her clients were Jewish, conservative but not practicing. Jim decided on a slow-braised brisket with new potatoes and roasted brussels sprouts. He kept the menu kosher even if his kitchen was not. His brisket braise was red wine based on rehydrated wild mushrooms. He used the same pinot noir that he planned to serve and added roasted garlic and fresh rosemary in the braise.

The dinner started with savory asparagus spring rolls with a kosher anchovy-based fish sauce. His salad was simple and lightly dressed. He added dried cherries and walnuts to his balsamic reduction. He offered dessert, his own baklava with a filo dough made with oil. He served a sweet Turkish coffee.

Jennifer was pleased and she let him know. He took the initiative and worked hard at making things right for her. Her guests asked if he was a private chef and could they hire him. She said no, he was a good friend who liked to cook for her.

Until that very moment, she had not considered the future of their relationship. He was submissive to her, and she enjoyed both his submission and the good things that came to her because of his submission. She felt he gave his consent in his willing participation, enjoying the purpose in life he found in her. From time to time, she liked putting him over her knee and he asked to go there. Videos of the canings he received were unusually satisfying to her. It was all good.

Far and away, the most gratifying part of their relationship was his chastity cage, both to her and, as she understood, to him. She kept the key locked up in a box on her nightstand next to her bed. Sometimes, when she brought a date into her bedroom and her bed, she touched that box. It heightened her pleasure.

He had become something more than a roommate or a friend. Her usual answer to the question about him no longer made sense. She had invested too much time and money in him for him to be her friend. When she worked long into the evening, he brought her a dinner he prepared for her. He took care of her home, her clothes, her shopping, her life. He had invested too much in her.

She prepared herself for the day Jim expressed regret or a desire for a different relationship, an end to his implied consent, or a desire for exclusive commitment. But it didn't happen. Instead, he suggested she call him her butler. [Her Butler Part 3] She understood the importance of his request: her butler, her servant, his life devoted to her. Greater commitment framed in submission to her.

The idea that Sundays would be on the honor system was hers. She wanted him to learn to defend himself and her. Security became a concern at her firm as they were embroiled in international conflicts over water rights and contractual obligations. James spent Sunday in martial arts and self-defense classes. Jennifer enjoyed feeling for his chastity device on Monday morning.

As an attorney, Jennifer often found herself defending positions with which she did not agree. Her sanctuary, her home, was there for her because James kept it that way. When they moved to Kenilworth, she had the means to make his job as her butler full-time. He took great pride in his position as her servant. She compensated him well.

The opportunity to lead the Strasbourg office was too good to pass up. The years in the EU were some of the best in her life, largely because her butler went with her. Besides their regular over her knee spankings, she enjoyed taking up the task of caning him. In return, he made her home an elegant oasis.

In the sacred moment of their only kiss at his bedside in the hospital, she told him she was glad she chose him all those years ago. For one awesome, holy moment, Jennifer was filled with love for this man who gave her a lifetime of enduring desire, submission, and unspoken consent.

He whispered to her, "Thank you, Mistress Agony." He smiled. She liked his smile. They were holding hands when he died.